CAT AND MOUSE

Phyllis Root ILLUSTRATED BY James Croft

Introduction

Before your child starts reading, read this story description. Then look through the book together and talk about the pictures.

This story is called *Cat and Mouse*. It's about how Mouse runs and how Cat runs after him. Cat chases Mouse under a fence and up a hill. When Cat tags Mouse, it's Mouse's turn to chase Cat!

Mouse runs.

Cat runs after Mouse.

Mouse runs under a fence.

Cat runs after Mouse.

Mouse runs up a hill.

Cat runs after Mouse.

Cat tags Mouse.

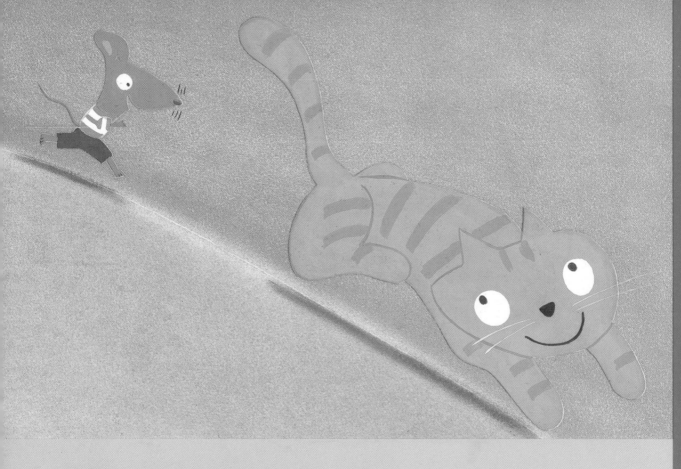

Mouse runs after Cat.

HELPING YOUR BRAND-NEW READER

Here's how to make first-time reading easy and fun:

▶ Read the introduction at the beginning of the book aloud. Look through the pictures together so that your child can see what happens in the story before reading the words.

▶ Read one or two pages to your child, placing your finger under each word.

▶ Let your child touch the words and read the rest of the story. Give him or her time to figure out each new word.

▶ If your child gets stuck on a word, you might say, *"Try something. Look at the picture. What would make sense?"*

▶ If your child is still stuck, supply the right word. This will allow him or her to continue to read and enjoy the story. You might say, *"Could this word be 'ball'?"*

▶ Always praise your child. Praise what he or she reads correctly, and praise good tries too.

▶ Give your child lots of chances to read the story again and again. The more your child reads, the more confident he or she will become.

▶ Have fun!

Text copyright © 2002 by Phyllis Root
Illustrations copyright © 2002 by James Croft

First edition 2002

ISBN 978-0-7636-1359-4

BNR *Mouse Has Fun*

20 SWT 25 24

Printed in Dongguan, Guangdong, China

This book was typeset in Arta Medium.
The illustrations were done in
acrylic and pastel.

Candlewick Press
99 Dover Street
Somerville, Massachusetts 02144

www.candlewick.com

CANDLEWICK PRESS

1002

Learn more at www.brandnewreaders.com

Mouse is fast, but Cat is faster!

Includes advice to help you guide and
support your brand-new reader.

PICNIC

Phyllis Root ILLUSTRATED BY James Croft

Introduction

Before your child starts reading, read this story
description. Then look through the book together
and talk about the pictures.

This story is called *Picnic*. It's about
how Mouse finds cookies, apples, bread,
cheese, and strawberries. Then he finds
Dog. Dog finds a bone. So Mouse
and Dog have a picnic.

Mouse finds cookies.

Mouse finds apples.

Mouse finds bread.

Mouse finds cheese.

Mouse finds strawberries.

Mouse finds Dog.

Dog finds a bone.

Mouse and Dog have a picnic.

HELPING YOUR BRAND-NEW READER

Here's how to make first-time reading easy and fun:

▶ Read the introduction at the beginning of the book aloud. Look through the pictures together so that your child can see what happens in the story before reading the words.

▶ Read one or two pages to your child, placing your finger under each word.

▶ Let your child touch the words and read the rest of the story. Give him or her time to figure out each new word.

▶ If your child gets stuck on a word, you might say, *"Try something. Look at the picture. What would make sense?"*

▶ If your child is still stuck, supply the right word. This will allow him or her to continue to read and enjoy the story. You might say, *"Could this word be 'ball'?"*

▶ Always praise your child. Praise what he or she reads correctly, and praise good tries too.

▶ Give your child lots of chances to read the story again and again. The more your child reads, the more confident he or she will become.

▶ Have fun!

Not for individual sale.

Text copyright © 2002 by Phyllis Root
Illustrations copyright © 2002
by James Croft

All rights reserved.

First edition 2002

ISBN 978-0-7636-1360-0

BNR *Mouse Has Fun*

20 SWT 25 24

Printed in Dongguan, Guangdong, China

This book was typeset in Arta Medium.
The illustrations were done in acrylic and pastel.

Candlewick Press
99 Dover Street
Somerville, Massachusetts 02144

www.candlewick.com

CANDLEWICK PRESS

1002

Learn more at www.brandnewreaders.com

BRAND
NEW
READERS®

Mouse and Dog know how to find tasty treats!

Includes advice to help you guide and
support your brand-new reader.

IT'S SUPER MOUSE!

Phyllis Root   ILLUSTRATED BY James Croft

Introduction

Before your child starts reading, read this story
description. Then look through the book together
and talk about the pictures.

This story is called *It's Super Mouse!*
It's about how Mouse can jump off many
things, like a step, a box, a rock, and a
fence. But when he jumps off a hill,
he makes a crash landing.

It's Super Mouse!

Super Mouse jumps off a step.

Super Mouse jumps off a box.

Super Mouse jumps off a rock.

Super Mouse jumps off a fence.

Super Mouse jumps off a hill.

Super Mouse flies!

OOF! Super Mouse lands.

HELPING YOUR BRAND-NEW READER

Here's how to make first-time reading easy and fun:

▌ Read the introduction at the beginning of the book aloud. Look through the pictures together so that your child can see what happens in the story before reading the words.

▌ Read one or two pages to your child, placing your finger under each word.

▌ Let your child touch the words and read the rest of the story. Give him or her time to figure out each new word.

▌ If your child gets stuck on a word, you might say, *"Try something. Look at the picture. What would make sense?"*

▌ If your child is still stuck, supply the right word. This will allow him or her to continue to read and enjoy the story. You might say, *"Could this word be 'ball'?"*

▌ Always praise your child. Praise what he or she reads correctly, and praise good tries too.

▌ Give your child lots of chances to read the story again and again. The more your child reads, the more confident he or she will become.

▌ Have fun!

Text copyright © 2002 by Phyllis Root
Illustrations copyright © 2002 by James Croft

All rights reserved.

First edition 2002

ISBN 978-0-7636-1361-7

BNR *Mouse Has Fun*

20 SWT 25 24

Printed in Dongguan, Guangdong, China

This book was typeset in Arta Medium.
The illustrations were done in
acrylic and pastel.

Candlewick Press
99 Dover Street
Somerville, Massachusetts 02144

www.candlewick.com

CANDLEWICK PRESS

1002

Learn more at www.brandnewreaders.com

BRAND NEW READERS®

Is it a bird?
Is it a plane?
No, it's Super Mouse!

**Includes advice to help you guide and
support your brand-new reader.**

PIZZA

Phyllis Root ILLUSTRATED BY James Croft

Introduction

Before your child starts reading, read this story description. Then look through the book together and talk about the pictures.

This story is called *Pizza*. It's about what happens when Mouse tries to cook toast, soup, and peas. When he burns the food, Mouse orders pizza.

Mouse makes toast.

The toast burns.

Mouse makes soup.

The soup burns.

Mouse makes peas.

The peas burn.

Mouse makes a phone call.

Pizza!

HELPING YOUR BRAND-NEW READER

Here's how to make first-time reading easy and fun:

◗ Read the introduction at the beginning of the book aloud. Look through the pictures together so that your child can see what happens in the story before reading the words.

◗ Read one or two pages to your child, placing your finger under each word.

◗ Let your child touch the words and read the rest of the story. Give him or her time to figure out each new word.

◗ If your child gets stuck on a word, you might say, *"Try something. Look at the picture. What would make sense?"*

◗ If your child is still stuck, supply the right word. This will allow him or her to continue to read and enjoy the story. You might say, *"Could this word be 'ball'?"*

◗ Always praise your child. Praise what he or she reads correctly, and praise good tries too.

◗ Give your child lots of chances to read the story again and again. The more your child reads, the more confident he or she will become.

◗ Have fun!

Text copyright © 2002 by Phyllis Root
Illustrations copyright © 2002 by James Croft

First edition 2002

ISBN 978-0-7636-1362-4

BNR *Mouse Has Fun*

20 SWT 25 24

Printed in Dongguan, Guangdong, China

This book was typeset in Arta Medium.
The illustrations were done in
acrylic and pastel.

Candlewick Press
99 Dover Street
Somerville, Massachusetts 02144

www.candlewick.com

CANDLEWICK PRESS

1002

Learn more at www.brandnewreaders.com

**BRAND
NEW
READERS**®

When Mouse burns his dinner, he knows just what to do!

**Includes advice to help you guide and
support your brand-new reader.**